A SUSPICIOUS COLLECTION

Dear Eliza,
Fill your life with stories
and make sure there are
a few suspicious ones!

Yenni.

WORLDCON 2019.

A SUSPICI♀US C♀LLECTI♀N
OF STORIES, POETRY, AND DRAWINGS

YEN ♀♀I

create
think
do

Cover and book design by Paola Pagano
Edited by Aki Schilz
All illustrations by Yen Ooi
ISBN: 978-1-910852-04-0

Table of Content

1

Can You

A life within
a life with a soul,
escaping
from this world
without even saying
hello.

Two hands entangled,
grasping for strength
to overcome the pain,
holding onto shared memory:
a feeling, an emptiness.

Palm to palm,
each reminding the other
they are here: we are here
now.

Darkness coming,
life going —
I'm dying, can you save me?
Light shining,
love breathing —
I'm living, can you feel me?

An earlier version was published in For Love and Poetry, *by Universe and Words, January 2013.*

2

The Starbucks Boy

This is the story of a good friend of mine. I have changed her name here to respect her privacy, even though she has passed on. She left me her diary and this is my story for her, of her.

Daniella Robertson was a tall, confident woman with a shocking head of red hair. She enjoyed a Starbucks coffee every day. As a freelance make-up artist, she had a relaxed schedule and could afford a long mid-morning break every day when she would walk to the Starbucks nearest to her house and have a Venti Caramel Latte. It was an early autumn day when she walked into Starbucks for her regular coffee and met a new man working behind the counter.

She was smitten at first sight. He was young — only nineteen — athletic, not too tall, tanned and very good looking. His slightly ruffled hair and cheeky smile drew out the youth in him. She described him in her diary as *a hot surfer boy with mixed Hawaiian-Japanese parents*. He was supporting his part-time college education through working at Starbucks. Having signed up for the morning shift every weekday, they inevitably saw a lot of each other.

Daniella couldn't help herself as she teased and flirted with him each day. Being still just a teenager, he blushed at her approaches and was too polite to rebuke her, secretly enjoying the attention as well. If he was at the till, she would always linger with her fingers on his palm as she gave him the cash. If he was serving the coffee, she would be cheeky and sit at a table instead of waiting for her coffee to be served like everyone else. Because she was a regular, the staff would bring the coffee to her, and soon it would always be him bringing the coffee to her.

Daniella knew that the other staff teased him endlessly about the attention she was giving him, but she enjoyed seeing him blush too much to care. She was under his spell and he didn't even know it.

On Tuesday mornings, when the shop was generally quiet, he took to bringing Daniella her coffee and even sitting down and having a quick casual chat with her. He had an air of confidence about him, but also a sense of naivety.

It was precisely a month from their first meeting when Daniella decided to make her move. From her diary entries, she had clearly not been able to stop thinking of him, and now she wanted more and was ready to make the first move. Near the end of her visit that day, he stopped by her table as he was going around the shop.

"Do you have a girlfriend?" she asked nonchalantly.

"No," he answered, as he blushed from his neck to the roots of his hair.

"Are you embarrassed talking about this with me?"

He fumbled, before saying, "Slightly... but I like it."

She smiled and reached out to touch his hand. He let it linger for a second before pulling away, looking around to see if anyone was looking at them.

"Do you know what's happening... what we're doing?" she asked him.

He nodded.

"Do you mind that I flirt with you?"

He shook his head and only just managed a whisper in reply. "I like it."

She smiled. "Thanks for being open with me. With the same honesty, do you think I'm pretty?"

He nodded more vigorously and smiled, encouraging her further.

She reached into her bag and pulled out a piece of paper. On it, she wrote her name, her mobile phone number and the name of a hotel nearby.

"Meet me tomorrow after the end of your shift. Text me and I'll reply with the room number. Is that ok?"

His eyes grew wide as he stared at her, unable to respond immediately.

"Just nod if you're OK with this."

He nodded.

"OK. I'll see you tomorrow." She smiled warmly and reassuringly as she gathered her things, her shaking hands betraying the excitement she felt.

~

Daniella did not go to Starbucks the next day, or any day after that. They met at the hotel as she had decided, and that was the beginning of their affair. Daniella wrote about the details of each visit and how they explored each other. It was slow but seemed to be a very satisfying relationship for the both of them. He was, however, a virgin when they first started, and not wanting to scare him off, Daniella kept it that way for the first few months, exploring other ways of pleasuring each other, teaching him, I guess, like Mrs Robinson. Hah, now that's funny. Mrs Robertson, Mrs Robinson. I wonder if Daniella ever thought of herself as the movie character.

They met once a week for nine months, both always looking forward to each meeting and never wanting to leave the room afterwards. He adored Daniella in the beginning, worshipped the ground she walked on, until he started to develop a stronger love for her, which reared its ugly but passionate head after the nine months. He asked her to marry him.

Daniella laughed the first time he asked.

"Why do you hurt me by laughing?" he asked her.

"You're so young, and I'm not exactly a spring chicken. People will talk."

"Do you care about what people will say about our love for each other?"

"No, my love. You are still young; you have your life ahead of you. I am just grateful that we have the chance for these moments together."

"So don't push me away. I might be young, but I know what I want."

"You think you know what you want now, but you won't be able to bear society laughing or looking down at you."

"Yes, I will. Anyway, they'll laugh at you too, so we'll both be laughed at together, which is fine with me."

"Me? Society has laughed at me all my life. I never belonged and they never understood. You, on the other hand, have never experienced anything like that."

He groaned into his hands as he realised that he wouldn't win the fight, not at that moment anyway, and dropped the matter. It was a few weeks later when he asked again, and then he didn't stop asking… until Daniella got ill.

~

"We can't see each other anymore."

"Why not?" he almost shouted, shaking from the fear of losing her.

"I'm ill. The doctors told me that I have cancer and it's very advanced. I only have a few months to live."

"Then let me stay by your side and help you through it."

"No. This is something I have to do by myself. I can't explain it and I won't."

"That's not fair," he sulked.

"I know," she said, as she laid a hand on his head and drew him close for one last embrace. "You have your life ahead of you. Please promise me you'll live it to the fullest and don't ever look back."

He started crying as she got up and left the room. She left him in the room alone that day and vowed never to see him again.

~

He got scared after two weeks when he couldn't reach Daniella on her mobile, and she didn't reply to any of his texts or messages. He realised that all he had of her was a name and the mobile number, which she promptly cancelled a few days later. He missed her and wanted to show her that he was mature enough to take care of her, like all the films that he had watched where the hero would go after the girl in the end and make things right. He wanted to make things right for her, especially for her last days.

He tried looking up more information about cancer to prepare himself, but he realised that it could be any kind of cancer and there were so many. Feeling helpless, he searched everywhere for a trace of her, but he couldn't find her in the telephone book or on the internet. He didn't know what to do, until one day he overheard a conversation by two people who came into Starbucks for a coffee.

They mentioned the name Daniella, cancer and the Red Cross Hospital. He kept quiet and didn't try to start a conversation or ask for more information, but it was after his shift that day that he went directly to the Red Cross Hospital.

At reception, he asked for Daniella Robertson and they told him that they didn't have any patients there by that name. Unsure about what else to do, he left for a walk and returned a while later when the receptionist had changed shifts to a different person. This time, he asked for the cancer department.

"Oh, you mean oncology?" the receptionist asked.

"Yes, thank you."

"It's on the fifth floor, just up those lifts through the doors," she said.

When he arrived at the department, he decided not to ask at the reception for Daniella, rather he went straight to the ward, to the patients' rooms. He started at a section where each room had four patients sharing the space. It was very quiet and all he heard were the machines pumping and beeping. His heart raced as he gathered his wits to check each room, staring into the faces of each patient to find Daniella.

Quietly, as he made his way, he finally found her. She was asleep on a bed by a window. She looked peaceful, but something wasn't right. It was her hair. She didn't have any. He took a deep breath as he reminded himself that cancer patients lost their hair in treatment, so this was normal. Feeling ridiculous and not knowing what to say to her, he kept quiet and let her sleep. He moved towards the foot of her bed and saw her patient's chart hanging off the end of it. Curious, he picked it up.

His eyes scanned the page, and on the top, it said: "Daniel Robertson @ Daniella Robertson". He looked at her again, bile rising at the back of his throat. His mouth shaped a "No" as he mustered more courage to have a further look. Further down the chart, it said: "Prostate cancer".

He was young; he had his life ahead of him.

He ran, not realising that he ran straight past me, standing in the doorway, holding on to my paper cup of Starbucks coffee.

3

Si(gh)nus

This high-pitched buzz,
these distorted harmonies
are like a soundtrack
subconsciously preparing me
for your arrival. You,
so quiet, seemingly harmless
yet so lethal. You.
Vision blurring,
as sight fails to focus
and the internal thud
like a heart beat-beating…
a build-up of pressure
like a cooker
but where

is the switch
to release this…
this…
Thoughts fail.
What is that sound?
If stars could sing
under water, it would,
yes it would, sound like
this high-pitched buzz.

4

Nine Lives

My cat, Chaney, was the only one who knew or cared that I was dead. Even I didn't care in the beginning. I just lay on my bed thinking that the naysayers were right after all, that the world had come to an end. Imagine my surprise when I got up and out of bed — probably on the third day, though I can't ever be sure, what with my brains already decomposing — to discover that I was physically dead.

Yes, I have since discovered that the dead have emotions. It's a bummer, but we don't really stop being who we are after we die. I don't know about those who pass over to the other side, or if there is another side, or heaven or hell. All I know is that I died and I am still here and I do not see other dead people around.

I was always a recluse, and Chaney was and still is my best friend. I found her in a ditch when she was barely a week old, all wet and with her eyes still closed. I heard her soft mewing while I was walking home from work one day and I knew that she was calling to me. Her first two nights were spent at the vet's on a drip, and it saved her life and cost me three hundred dollars. Well, that's not important anymore as Chaney proved to be much more than a pet for me. She is my one true companion, and now, my saviour. Funny how the roles have reversed.

Anyway, the night I died was a cool summer night. I had left all the windows opened, thinking that the breeze felt like silk, wrapping around my body. I came home from work at around six, as usual, fed Chaney while I ate my own dinner, and I watched some TV before bed. I don't know what happened and I guess I'll never find out, but I just didn't wake up the next morning. I remember either thinking or dreaming that the world had ended, with little remorse or sadness.

When I came to, I heard Chaney mewing really loudly, and my neighbours were shouting for her to stop. Thinking that I had missed her feed, I tried to bolt out of bed, but I ended up floating straight across the room. I saw my body for the first time, lying on the bed, being consumed by maggots and covered in flies. I read that it doesn't take long for an exposed body to decompose, and I guess I had been dead for a few days. Though I was shocked and horrified at the look of my own body, it was an odd feeling, as without a body, you don't really react. It just became a fact that I got over really quickly. I was more concerned that Chaney had not been fed yet.

Chaney was fine. With the window open, she was able to go out daily to an old lady that lives in the block across the road from us who puts out boiled fish for her. She probably eats better there, and I was glad. I was sad though, as I was stuck in my apartment with only my rotting corpse for company. I couldn't do anything with myself other than float around and wonder how to get out.

I guess because the windows were open, the smell wasn't a problem, and none of my neighbours were really bothered that they had not seen me in a while. Why should they when I didn't speak to them when I was alive. I tried leaving the apartment, but there seemed to be some kind of a barrier. Reaching through the open window just felt like the window was shut. I tested the edge of every wall in my apartment and it was the same. I was stuck.

∽

It was probably two or three months later — I don't know, you kinda lose track of time when you're dead — when I noticed that Chaney had got bigger. She would still come to the apartment every day and mew loudly, but no one took any notice. Otherwise, she would get on with her routine of sleeping in her favourite spots, scratching the sofa and chasing her catnip fish around each time. I was convinced she couldn't sense me at all. Well, not until that time about two or three months later.

Chaney came in and was cleaning herself in her favourite bed when she had suddenly sat upright and stared straight at where I was. I tried speaking — it's not a habit that's easy to break out of, even after you lose the ability to do anything physical — but even though nothing came out, I felt a kind of connection with Chaney, perhaps through my thoughts. She continued staring at me and then she purred.

I moved towards her and was pleased to sense that she was purring even more loudly, and she started rolling on her back, giving me the "stroke me" pose. It was frustrating watching her being so affectionate and unable to respond in any way, so I just stayed there as close to her as I could. She reached out with a paw and touched me. I thought I was life-size until that moment, and then I suddenly felt like I was just a ball. As she pulled at me with her paw; she pressed me against her belly, nuzzling me in her fuzzy soft fur.

I think the thought of being nuzzled in her belly was enough to make me feel safe and happy. I don't think I actually felt anything — as I physically couldn't feel — but it was a calming sensation. As I took in this new feeling, not only being able to communicate with Chaney, but also being able to be close to her, she grabbed me tighter, pushing me further in.

That was when I moved past her fur, past her skin. I found that there was a space inside her that I could fit in, wrapped up in the warmth of her womb, next to four other kittens. She was pregnant, she was carrying a litter of five and I was the fifth! Chaney had known that one of her kittens was a stillborn and she knew that I could use the dead foetus as a vessel and had come to collect me.

Chaney didn't waste any time. As soon as I was snugly inside her, she got up and made her way out of my apartment. I could somehow read her intentions and figured out what she was trying to do. I instinctively knew that she was helping me get out. She didn't go very far, just a few blocks away, to a local morgue. In the five years that I lived in that flat, I had no idea that we were so close to a morgue, or that a morgue could be located so centrally in a city. We sat just outside of an open window for quite a long time, before Chaney decided to make her way, squeezing between the window bars.

Chaney ran in like she knew the place well and quickly picked out her target. There was a fresh corpse on a metallic table in front of us. She jumped straight onto the dead body, and that was when I thought I heard her speak in my thoughts. It was the only time Chaney ever spoke — I think — and it was a very rough "get out!"

I pushed my way out and found that I had gone from Chaney's womb straight into the body on the table. I lay there, taking in the feeling of actually lying down, when I felt Chaney's wet nose rubbing at my hand. Yes, it was my hand and I could feel it!

I sat up and found that it was no different to when I was alive, in my own body, except that this body was a little bigger… and male.

Chaney jumped off the metallic table and growled at me, which was when I heard the sounds of men talking in the other room. They were moving towards us and I guess Chaney wanted us to leave quickly. Without thinking, I followed Chaney and she led us to a back door in the building, which I was able to open with my hands! I smiled as I felt the warmth of the sun hitting my new face as we walked down the street. I felt free again, but that was until I caught my reflection off a shop window. I was a guy now, over six feet tall and looking quite dead. I was now grey and dull, looking like a zombie.

That was when it hit me. I was a zombie.

I started to panic. There were people walking around me on this busy street and someone would surely realise that I was a walking dead body. I looked around in fear and realised that Chaney had been sat by my feet all this while. As I looked at Chaney, she started walking, leading me to quiet back streets, weaving through the city until we came away from everything. She brought us to the entrance of an old monsoon drain where we could shelter and were away from prying eyes. She is a genius.

~

Chaney takes care of herself. She goes on her own to shops and restaurants that will offer her food, and she comes back to be with me and to take care of me. She had her litter of kittens not long after, and I got to watch her tend to them, teach them survival skills and let them go when they were ready. I helped her bury the little fifth kitten that had helped me escape.

She gave her kittens to a good home at the edge of the city one night. She picked up one of the kittens and had motioned for me to follow, so I picked up the other three and walked with her until we reached a beautiful tree-lined suburban housing area with large bungalows. Chaney went straight to a beautiful bungalow that had a swing in the front and a massive tree with a treehouse in the garden, and she dropped the kitten on the doorstep. I followed suit and put the other three on the doorstep too. Chaney jumped onto a bench next to the door and tried to reach for the doorbell. I realised what she was trying to do and helped. After we rang the doorbell, the both of us left the house quickly and hid in a nearby bush. We watched as a beautiful woman carrying a crying baby opened the door.

The baby stopped crying as soon as he saw the kittens, and the woman smiled. She called out and a young girl came out to the door a few minutes later with a basket to collect the kittens and took them into the house.

Chaney rubbed herself on my legs and walked away. We never saw the kittens again, but Chaney didn't seem to mind.

∿

My body didn't last too long. It still decomposes even though I'm in it, so I guess that really makes me the walking dead. It's not a problem for me, as thankfully I can't smell and I have lost interest in vanity. I rely on Chaney to let me know when I need to change bodies.

We travel by foot, Chaney and I, walking from city to city, moving from morgue to morgue. We borrow dead bodies of all kinds. I have been in a fox, a squirrel and even a bird, but I don't stay long in animal bodies as I can't control them as well.

I don't know what I'll do when Chaney dies. Perhaps I will be able to pass over to the other side, or go to heaven, though I don't think heaven can be any better than what I have right now: a simple life, travelling with my best friend.

First published in Eat, *a collection of zombie stories by Spectacle Publishing Media Group, September 2012.*

5

Rain

That night, the rain came down hard and heavy, like a continuous dark curtain that was determined to drench anything in its way, and she was in its way. Her Victorian costume felt like it weighed a tonne as she dragged it to the bus stop. She held her wig in her hand, the grisly fake hairs between her fingers reminding her of the dish scourer she had been using nearly twelve hours ago. Her white Victorian make-up ran down her face against the black mascara and eyeliner. She knew that she looked like a horror, worse than when she had arrived at the Halloween party earlier. As she thought about the party, she smiled to herself — despite the rain — thinking about the handsome vampire whom she had allowed under her many layers of lace.

As she dragged herself to the bus stop, she stared as far as she could on both sides of the road, trying to get a glimpse of any vehicles. She could see nothing and resigned herself to the uncomfortable red bench that was at least shading some of the rain. She cursed herself for not leaving the party earlier, waiting until she was the last one standing — though she needed support with standing by that time — before she let herself out of her friend's flat. Knowing that she'd probably be at the bus stop for a while, she started to inspect the damage the rain had done.

She balanced her wig and purse on the sloped bench, before she stood up and attempted to wring her dress dry, bit by bit. Still feeling drunk but happy, she swayed as she worked through the many layers of her dress, her back to the road. She smiled, staring at her own reflection in the glass panel before letting her eyes drop back to the bench.

"Fuck!" she shouted out, her voice shocking her more than anything else. She reached for her purse as she spotted that it was open and checked its contents. Everything was in there except for her Oyster card. "Crap," she said out loud again; this time she was more prepared to hear herself. "Oh fuck, I can't even take the bloody bus, can I? They don't accept fucking money anymore, bloody TFL." She chattered happily to herself, feeling secluded by the wall of rain around her.

"May I be of service, milady?" she heard a male voice rasp as she jumped around to face a shrivelled old man with hardly any teeth, smiling at her.

"Oh, fuck, sorry, fuck." She shook her head in an attempt to sober up a little more as she composed herself. "So sorry, I didn't see you."

"You seem to be in a spot of bother," he said, every "s" coming out as a whistle between the gaps in his teeth.

"Huh? Oh, yeah. I've dropped my bloody Oyster card, haven't I?" she said, realising that she was still somewhat drunk.

He continued smiling at her as he nodded in understanding and walked over to a red telephone box that now only tourists used as a photo prop, before reaching in and plucking a card out of the many that lined its glass walls.

She watched as he moved slowly through the rain, back into the bus stop, still smiling.

"Do you have something that I could write with?" he asked her.

"Erm... hang on," she said as she reached into her purse, digging around to have a look. She found her eyeliner, which had cost her a bomb, but she wasn't in any state to argue with herself, so she handed it over to the old man.

"Thank you," he wheezed.

She could see that he was holding a card with a picture of a scantily clad woman on the front and a mobile number printed in bold across it. She smiled, as it reminded her of her earlier encounter. She struggled to remember the vampire's name and decided that he would be Bram in her memory now, as she gave herself a little chuckle.

The old man broke her reverie as he placed the card into her hand. His skin was so cold to the touch that it gave her goose pimples. She looked at him in confusion as he smiled and gave her a bow, before walking out into the rain once again. Her gaze followed his path as he walked past the telephone box and into the blackness that seemed to have enveloped him.

She looked down to her hand that was grasping the card. On the front, where the woman was posed seductively, he had scribbled across it with her eyeliner, "Oyster". She turned the card around, and on the white back, there were other words written with her eyeliner, mostly smudged. She stared more closely and could make out the start of the first two lines, which said, "The issue and use of this Oyster car—" and "copies of which are available at tfl.g—"

At that moment, she could hear a vehicle approaching, and she turned to see a red bus trundling along. She waved as the driver pulled the bus to a stop, leaving her standing right in front of the door. She turned to gather her things from the bench and then stepped into the brightly lit bus. She smiled at the bus driver, who was clearly used to seeing all sorts on the night route.

She started spurting out excuses at the driver, pleading for him to let her ride for free because she had lost her card in the rain, and telling him that he could have the fare in cash, but the driver stopped her in mid-flow and said, "But you're holding your Oyster card in your hand?"

Time seemed to slow for her as she raised her hand, card between her thumb and index finger, the wig hanging off the other fingers. She held the dodgy card up to the driver and asked, "This?"

He said, "That's your Oyster card, isn't it?"

She stood there with her mouth agape.

"Look lady, it's been a long night. Stop pissing about and just put the card up to the reader."

Not knowing what else to do, she moved the card towards the Oyster card reader, staring, as the woman sprawled across the card seemed to be smiling at her. As it reached the reader, it beeped, and she jumped. She looked up at the display: "Taken: £1.40, Balance: £999,998.60".

The bus jerked, starting, as she asked the driver, "Did you see that?"

"What?" he asked, clearly annoyed with her.

"My balance."

They both glanced at the machine again, but the display had cleared.

"Go sit down, please," the driver said, exasperated.

Defeated and confused, she moved through the

empty bus and took a seat at the back. She moved to put the card in her purse when she saw that it was now blue and made of plastic. The woman in the skimpy lingerie was no longer there. Instead, a brand new Oyster card sat between her fingers — fingers that were still stained with black kohl.

6

Death

She waits patiently,
never rushing, never hurrying,
never asking either. She picks —
not favourites, not at random —
she just picks from a list Fate gave her
and takes them.

They go with her,
sometimes fighting, sometimes willingly
but always they go,
                to a better place,
                                to an unknown
place.

And those who are left behind?
They mourn.

7

Two Strangers

The tunnel to hell, I remember thinking cynically as I stepped on the walkway to board the 2.30 p.m. to New York. I hate flying. Twenty-eight, and I have still not got over my fear of flying. At least I got my favourite seat. Smack in the middle near the front. As always, I placed my hand luggage in the overhead compartment, only holding on to my book and a bottle of water.

"Sorry," he said. "Do you mind moving in a bit? I'm sitting here too, but there are people behind me waiting to get through."

His voice was like a dream. With just a slight accent and perfect enunciation.

"Sure." I shuffled into my seat and beamed at him. I felt like an idiot.

Perfectly tanned skin, his hair was dark brown, kept short and tidy. He wore slightly baggy jeans and a very baggy hoody. The top was clearly too big for him. With the sleeves rolled up, I could tell that he wasn't a big guy.

"You headed to New York too?" I asked, immediately realising how silly I sounded. We were on the same flight after all.

"Umm... yeah."

I smiled and busied myself with my seat belt and pillow.

"Sorry, I'm just a bit nervous," he said.

"Oh! Don't worry, I am too. I have a fear of flying." I giggled, trying to hide the fear in my voice.

"Fear of flying? Wow!"

I stared at his lovely face. His perfect nose.

"I've never met anyone who had a fear of flying. I'm just nervous 'cause I've never been to The Big Apple."

Blushing, I looked down at my fingers and started fiddling with my seat belt again.

"Sorry, I didn't mean to make you even more nervous. Please let me know if there's anything I can do to help you with your... umm... condition."

"It's OK. It's taken me more than ten years of practice, but I can just about manage a two-hour flight now."

He smiled. His eyes seemed to twinkle.

The plane took off and I was too distracted about

embarrassing myself even more to be scared. I tried reading for a bit, but it was more like holding the book to my nose and trying not to peek at him. I was relieved when the stewardess brought us some water and juice. We both took the juice.

"My name is Mary, by the way," I said.

"Oh... hi, Mary. I'm Yakob."

"Hey, Yakob."

We smiled. I thought I saw him blush.

"Umm, so why are you headed to New York?" he asked.

"Oh, I was actually visiting my parents. New York is home, if you can believe it."

"That must be so cool. Living in the big city."

He seemed to drift off into his own thoughts. It was then that I saw him patting his chest, as if he had a passport or money pouch underneath. I must have been staring, as he caught my eyeline and looked down at his hand, quickly retracting it.

"What about you?" I blurted. I was desperate to keep the conversation going.

"I'm visiting some friends."

"College mates? First trip alone?" I asked.

He laughed. It was a genuine hearty laugh, which brought a big smile to my face.

"Do I really look that young?"

Before I could say anything, he stopped me.

"Don't answer that," he grinned. "I'm thirty-two and left college more than ten years ago."

"I'm so sorry. You must get that all the time though... right?"

"Yeah, and don't worry. I'm used to it."

"Well, since you told me your age, I guess it's only good manners to tell you mine. I'm twenty-eight."

"Well, hello Mary who is twenty-eight years old. It's very nice to meet you," he said as he stuck out a hand to shake mine.

We shook hands and started laughing at the ridiculous situation we'd got ourselves into.

The next hour was pure bliss. We chatted like old friends about everything under the sun. I don't know why, but I found Yakob so easy to talk to, and I guess the feeling was mutual, for he was telling me about his very conservative parents from the Middle East. They seemed like suffocating parents, but then again, whose parents aren't?

～

We will shortly be making our descent...

I can't remember what we were talking about at that exact moment, but Yakob stopped in mid-sentence and froze. He looked like he had just seen a ghost. I couldn't get him to tell me what was wrong. He stood up abruptly and went straight to the toilet. I guessed that he was feeling ill.

I started to get up after him but my fear kicked in as

I became painfully aware of the plane engines rumbling. Suddenly, everything started spinning, and the last thing I heard were gasps from the people sitting around me, as everything blurred into one black patch which shrunk into a dot and disappeared into whiteness.

I could still hear, but I could neither move, nor speak, nor see.

~

"Mary! Mary!" It was Yakob.

I felt a surge of warmth through my body, relieved to know that he was fine.

"Come on, Mary. Can you hear me?"

I wanted to say yes, but I couldn't. There was a lot of movement around me and I heard someone say that he was a doctor and to let him through. I felt the arms around me change, as I was being propped up. The floor sounded like it was opening up. There was a loud screech, which I realised later was the landing gear engaging. I heard a deep voice saying my name, and suddenly a smell hit me, and my eyes opened with a start – smelling salts. I looked around frantically and found Yakob crouched by my feet with his face in his hands.

I wanted to grab his hand, but still weak, I just stroked him instead. He looked up at me. He looked confused at first, but then a smile slowly spread across his face. The doctor moved away and let Yakob come around to me.

Surprisingly, we had landed.

I hugged Yakob and started crying openly. Relieved. It was then that I started realising that the other passengers were staring at us and a few of them were even clapping. Thoroughly embarrassed, we both sat back in our seats holding hands and quietly absorbing the situation while the other passengers got out of the plane.

"I'm really sorry," he said.

"What for? I was the one who fainted." I chuckled nervously.

"I'll tell you one day, but right now, I just want to say thank you."

Confused, I just smiled and held his hands tighter.

Yakob came to stay with me that day, and it's now five years later and he still hasn't left. It took him more than a year before he would tell me the truth, which I have fully forgiven him for. When he was patting his chest on the flight that day, he was actually checking for a small explosive device.

8

The Empty Bed

They had arrived together. We heard about the news and that they were being transferred to us, but we didn't ask any further. It seemed that they were not talking to anyone about what had happened anyway. The police had wanted to continue investigations but the Senior Citizens' Party managed to put a stop to it.

Alexander Whiting was seventy-six and Belinda Baskerville was seventy-nine at the time. I was a newly hired receptionist, straight out of university and happy to have my first job and first pay cheque.

Since then, the home has grown in size, with over 200 residents on site now and more than enough carers, housekeepers, medics and nurses to cope. I am now managing the reception team of five. Reception Manager.

Anyway, this story is not about me, nor about the Copperfield Nursing Home. It is a story that Alex and Bel and thirty-two others had kept a secret for sixteen years.

~

When Alex and Bel first arrived, they kept to themselves, never speaking to anyone else. They answered doctors and nurses with nods or head shakes alone. We knew that they could speak, as when left alone, they would whisper surreptitiously between themselves.

We were given strict instructions by management that they were not to be questioned about the incident at all. It seemed that the Senior Citizens' Party made that a condition for their accommodation at the home. We respected their privacy, and in turn, they gradually trusted us enough to be comfortable in their new home. They still only uttered the odd word or two.

We used to think that Alex and Bel were involved with each other, as they were inseparable. We soon realised, however, that theirs was a sort of alliance or partnership, which we now know spanned out of a shared secret. A burden of sorts.

They were both very healthy, physically able and never needed any support or help. They had no complaints, either, and the doctors were always pleased with them after their medical tests. They loved walking in the woods behind the home, which provided more than enough exercise for their age.

Alex died at eighty-nine years old, three years ago now, due to a lung failure. It was old age that took him, really. Bel was naturally distraught. She waited another three years before leaving us in April, earlier this year. Her heart gave up. It was quick.

We think that Bel knew her time was up, as it was Easter when she took us by surprise and asked to visit the church. We asked her why, and she said that she had a confession to make. She didn't volunteer more information and we respected her request.

The weather turned cold and she was poorly on the day, so we asked for the local priest to do a house call instead. She frequently visits the home to chat with many of our residents, but she had never spoken with Bel before.

It was a clear crisp day when she came to see Bel. I remember bringing her through to Bel's room.

"Morning, Belinda. My name is Jane Salmon. Pleased to meet you."

"Hi Jane... call me Bel. Thank you for coming all the way to see a dying old woman," Bel had said with a chuckle.

"Anytime. I am always at your service."

They hit it off straight away. I was glad to see Jane settled in and a little shocked to hear Bel speak so much. Curious as I was, I turned to head back to my duties. That was when Bel called for me to stay. She wanted a second pair of ears, was what she said. I asked Jane if it was alright and checked that the reception was covered before I settled into the Lazy Boy placed by the foot of Bel's bed.

Bel looked so small in her bed, swallowed up by the three white pillows and duvet around her. Jane sat in a chair next to the bed and reached out to hold Bel's hand as they spoke.

"So, Bel, I heard that you wanted a chat. Anything specific on your mind?"

"I am nearly ninety-five, Jane," Bel said as she looked across the room to the empty bed. It was Alex's bed.

"I have spent the last sixteen years thinking about what Alex and I did at that other home. I never stopped thinking, and I know Alex never stopped thinking about what happened either." Her hands started shaking, and we could see that she was getting uncomfortable.

Jane was clearly more experienced with these situations than I was. She just took both of Bel's hands in hers and looked directly into her eyes while I fidgeted uncomfortably.

"Take your time, Bel. We aren't going anywhere,

and I am sure that we have more than enough tea and biscuits for us to stay here for days," Jane said, smiling gently.

Bel took a deep breath and managed to calm herself before continuing.

"Let me start from the beginning," Bel said as she plunged us into the story of their lives.

Belinda Baskerville was already married at the age of twenty-four when she met Alexander Whiting. He was only twenty-one then, and the world was his oyster. She was working as a waitress in a restaurant which he frequented, as he had started an apprenticeship with a cobbler whose shop was only a few doors away.

Belinda, married to Norton Baskerville, a school teacher, had thought that her life was boring and unfulfilled. Though married for over three years, they hadn't had any children, which seemed to put a strain on the marriage.

Alex, on the other hand, had been trying his hand at all sorts. He worked as an apprentice to a barber, then a butcher, then a plumber, before he decided that cobbling was his new trade. At twenty-one, Alex stood at a strapping five feet eleven inches with a head full of beautiful golden-blond hair and sparkling blue eyes. He always seemed to be without a worry in the world.

Bel had served Alex a few times at the restaurant, and she was automatically taken by him. Bel felt energised every time Alex was around, and in the end she decided to make a move. She had heard all about Alex's encounters with the local girls and thought that she could get away with an affair with him.

It was a clear summer's day when Bel brazenly handed Alex a tissue with a time and address written on it in red. Her heart was beating so hard that she thought she was going to faint. After she gave Alex the tissue, she made some excuse and stayed in the kitchen until Alex left the restaurant.

She had given him the address of her friend's flat whom she was flat-sitting for at that time. Her friend, Angie, was visiting her family and was away for two weeks.

Bel ran to the flat and sat thinking for the longest time if she had gone mad. She freshened up and put on a nice silk slip that she had also borrowed from her friend, and then proceeded to sit and wait. Many things went through her mind at that time. She thought he was not going to turn up and started thinking about why she was so stupid, thinking why such a handsome young man would ever consider her over all the pretty young girls who threw themselves at him. She had just about given up when she heard knocking on the door.

Her stomach did a flip as she got up to answer it.

He had come after all.

They did not speak at all and left all the communicating to their physical needs. Afterwards, they curled up together, still not talking for as long as they could, before they dressed in silence and headed back to their separate homes. She swore that it was going to be a one-off and thought that she was never going to see him again.

The next day, Bel did not know this at the time, but Alex was called back to his family as his father had been in an accident. The news was not good and it was two weeks later when his father died.

Alex stayed with his family for two years, helping his mother and two sisters manage the household. He told Bel that he had thought of her throughout those years but did not know how he could contact her, for he did not even know her name.

Bel had assumed that Alex had left for greener pastures, never to return. With a heavy heart, she vowed to work on her marriage. Bel and Norton continued to be hopeful that she may get pregnant, so life went on as usual.

In the two years, Alex's sister, Mabel, got married to a well-off gentleman who took his mother and sister Alice with them to stay. So, Alex decided to move to the city to start a new life.

He was curious to see if Bel was still working at the restaurant and went to look for her before his move to the city. He wanted to see if fate had been kind.

Alex arrived at the restaurant one Monday morning and sat down to have a coffee when he saw Bel walk through to start her shift. Bel did not see him and walked straight through to the back. Alex, not knowing what to do, quickly scribbled his name and the name of the B&B that he was staying at on a napkin and waited until Bel came out. She did not even get the chance to look at him when he thrust the napkin into her palm and whispered, "Please come."

That was how their year-long affair started.

Alex had some money from his inheritance, and with odd errands that he ran for people here and there, he managed to maintain a small studio near the restaurant. Bel visited his flat every day and their relationship flourished.

～

It was a year later that Norton discovered the affair. He was home early one day and had wanted to surprise Bel at the restaurant when he saw her walking out, clearly having finished her shift. Norton followed Bel to Alex's flat and barged in on them.

Norton was delirious with anger. Feeling betrayed and having never met Alex or known of his existence, Norton decided to take his anger out on Bel.

Norton reached for the nearest thing he could find,

which was an umbrella propped against the door frame. As he reached over his head with the umbrella, ready to bring it down on Bel, Alex jumped in to protect her and got the brunt of the hit. This made Norton even angrier as he continued to bash the umbrella blindly at the both of them.

Alex somehow managed to crawl towards the kitchen and found a knife. Without thinking, he slashed at Norton, cutting him on his arms. There was blood everywhere.

Norton started using the umbrella even more aggressively, and that was when Alex stabbed the knife into his stomach. Norton crumpled to the ground and time stopped. There was silence as both Bel and Alex looked on in disbelief.

Alex placed the knife down on the floor and moved towards the telephone to call emergency services when Bel shouted in despair and reached out for the knife. Alex had thought that Bel was going to kill herself and abandoned the call, but instead, she reached over and killed Norton with a stab into his neck.

Bel turned to look at Alex with frenzied eyes and in a coarse whisper said, "The blood is on both our hands now. I will not let them take you alone. I want us to be together."

They called the police and confessed to the murder and the affair. The court ruled that it was not a planned murder but had started as self-defence. They were both given fifteen years in prison.

~

Over the fifteen years, they wrote to each other every day, keeping the other going with thoughts of meeting up on the outside. They stopped all communications with their families, who, after a while, had taken them for dead. Day by day, they lived their lives inside, keeping to themselves and not causing any trouble.

They were both pardoned only a month apart, and when they were released, they moved to the next county together, still keeping only to themselves. They worked odd jobs until they had saved enough money to buy a small plot of land and then they started farming. Organic farm produce started to become the fashion at that point, which meant that their business flourished. They sold their produce at their local supermarkets and maintained a quiet life until they were in their sixties.

It was the prison time that changed their relationship from lovers to partners. They were as inseparable as before, but they had both changed. Neither could not live without the other, but at the same time they were content with a platonic relationship.

~

About twenty-eight years ago, Bel and Alex realised that they should retire as they were getting old. They had enough money saved up, and with the proceeds from the sales of the farm, they could pay for their places at a nursing home. They looked at various places and decided to move to a county four hours away, to a cosy little home called "The Haven".

At The Haven, Bel and Alex could put their past behind them and started making friends again. The other residents warmed to them and immediately took them in as part of the family. Bel and Alex did not mind that the others were very religious and had even joined in with prayers and celebrations. They were finally happy and at peace.

~

It started about a year before the incident. The residents were holding more religious meetings. They talked about the idea of achieving ultimate peace through death.

Bel and Alex did not take part in the beginning, but started to pick up on more and more of the discussions as the other residents got more excited. They were all careful not to let any of The Haven's staff suspect anything as they started to plot.

The aim was for everyone to achieve ultimate peace

together, as one. They knew that Bel and Alex did not believe as they did, but they offered the choice to them anyway. Bel and Alex declined, as they did not think it was the right thing for them, but they wanted to help their new family. They started being more active in the discussions, and in the end, they got in too deep. They came up with a plan to help their thirty-two best friends achieve their goal.

~

"It was really easy, actually," said Bel.

"We rigged the work charts and used The Haven's office emails to let everyone know not to come in to work. No one questioned it as it seemed official, coming from The Haven office. We personalised the emails, letting each person know that their shift was covered and that there was just a mix-up in that week's schedule."

Bel intermittently stopped to gaze outside, as if to recall something. Her eyes were clear and her face emotionless.

"We pumped a room full of gas and we set up a spark starter which could be controlled from the other end of the building. After we said our goodbyes, the others grouped together in the gassed room to say a prayer while Alex and I, hand-in-hand, strolled slowly to the other end of the building. We knew that when we set off that trigger most of the others would have passed out from the gas anyway. We also wanted to make sure that there were no survivors... as that would have been torture," Bel whispered, and shuddered at the thought.

The room was silent as Bel continued to stare into space, as if in a trance.

Jane broke the silence with a question. "Why did you and Alex do it, Bel?"

Bel turned to look at Jane directly. Slowly, her lips twitched into a smile. It was a warm smile, one of age and experience.

"We did it because we wanted to repent."

This was when she laughed. Bel laughed a hearty laugh that made us really confused.

"I would have never thought that I would say this, but I was really naïve, even at the ripe old age of seventy-nine. Alex and I both thought that since we had already sinned before, we would be the ideal candidates for the role. We also thought that if we could help thirty-two people, the guilt of murdering one would fade away. Little did we know." Bel paused and softly shook her head.

"We couldn't talk about it for the longest time. In fact, we never did. It was only when Alex was suffering with his lungs that he told me that he wanted the truth out. He knew that it was not fair for the news to come out when I was still alive, so he gave me the choice, of telling it, or not, when I knew it was time.

Alex was right, of course. We sinned and we sinned twice. We covered the one murder with thirty-two more. It was not right, but how were we to know?" she said with regret in her voice.

"They were so sure of what they were doing that we believed and trusted them. We were naive," she sniggered to herself bitterly.

Jane looked at Bel with confidence in her eyes. She said, "It was not your fault, nor your guilt to bear, Bel. What you and Alex did, you did with pure innocent hearts. You have already done your time for the first mistake. What happened at The Haven was a choice that the others had made, not you."

Bel looked up at Jane, the years showing on the lines of her face. "Thank you, Jane. You comfort an old lady, but I know what we did."

~

Jane and I could not get Bel to say another word after that. She would smile at us or nod or shake her head, but she would not say another word until the day she passed on.

Jane and I went to the police with Bel's story after that, and they checked out all the facts. There were records of Bel's and Alex's time in prison and records of their daily letters being sent. The police also went through the records of all the thirty-two residents in

The Haven to see if there were any surviving relatives, but there were none.

So, where does that leave this story?

It is just that, just another story, which if it had been left untold would not have mattered anyway.

9

A Moment With You

It was as if I was never truly alive
until we met that late spring morning,
unplanned.

As usual I was mulling
when you approached,
bringing light into my life,
unaware you were my catalyst:
you started a chain reaction,
overloading my sensory perceptions —
I began to feel that
what was a dream or reality
did not matter when I saw, felt, tasted…
lived!

The depth of colour
The energy of life
The beauty of nature
all coming together
in a burst of emotions
so real, but indescribable:
like a song of nature
with lyrics of love.

10

Life-Stills™

❝ Thank you for participating in the clinical trials for Life-Stills™."

Sia had not combed her hair since it was last washed a week ago and the nurse did her best to remain professional, only wrinkling her nose slightly as she signed Sia in.

Sia shrugged. She was only there because her doctor had forced her to go. Really, she was happier at home, contemplating death.

"Sia Robson. Twenty-five. 32 Chiswick High Road. Is that right?"

Sia nodded this time, looking down at her shoes. Marc had bought them for her, but he was gone now.

"Please go to Meeting Room 3," the nurse said,

pointing at a door not too far away, "Where the introductions will start. Thank you."

Still looking at her feet, Sia dragged her pair of soiled Onitsuka Tigers along the floor, and headed towards the room she had been shown. She considered heading to the toilets and hanging herself there. Her shoelaces might be strong enough.

There was a hand at her elbow now, nudging her along. She let herself be led and only looked to see who it was once she was safely seated in a corner, away from people. How she despised people after the incident.

It was her doctor, Dr Clare Holloway, who smiled reassuringly at Sia before leaving her to find other patients.

The doors to the room were shut before it was full. There were as many patients as there were doctors and nurses. Not many in all. Sia was glad, as she could remain alone in the corner. She tried to listen to the introductions, but found her attention distracted by the tree outside.

The tree swayed alone and seemed to gesture at Sia to come out. Sia wanted to smile at the tree, but she didn't know how to; she felt her cheek muscles twitch. She shook her head sadly at the tree, as if it could understand her predicament, and turned to the doctor on stage.

He was talking about Life-Stills™, a new revolutionary mind-drug that would allow patients to re-live a moment in time, through physical feelings. A recent 'happy' moment for the patient is determined and scientists take a snapshot of the chemical make-up of the body in that moment, using a strand of the patient's hair. This chemical make-up is then copied into Life-Stills™ in the form of small circular dissolvable stickers. When placed on the patient's tongue, the drug acts as a catalyst to bring the body's chemicals and hormones to the precise state of the selected moment. The patient's body thus recreates the moment of physical happiness experienced in the snapshot, and will remain in this state for about half an hour before the drug wears off.

Sia had heard this explanation from Clare numerous times. It sounded far-fetched, and frankly, she didn't care. She'd agreed in her last session with Clare to try the drug, just once, though she was starting to have second thoughts. Clare had suggested she choose her wedding day as the moment to return to, as a way of recapturing the last happy moments before she fell into her depression. In truth, Sia hoped that reliving her wedding day might make her even more depressed and finally give her enough courage to take her own life. It was after all, the day before Marc died.

She looked outside again, but the tree had stopped swaying. It seemed to be throwing a tantrum, looking away.

The six patients were ushered to a desk where their prescriptions of Life-Stills™ were handed to them. They each got six doses and were given the choice to take their first dose at the hospital, or at home, though they would need to have someone with them.

Sia took her strip of stickers and left. She walked past the tree and said sorry to it, but it didn't reply. She walked home automatically, not thinking about where her feet were taking her.

Her home was a two-bed flat at the end of the high street. It was sparsely furnished, with boxes of wedding gifts still in various stages of unwrapping. They reminded her of Marc, which was painful, but she had thought it would be worse without them around.

Sia went straight to the couch and lay on it. Reaching into her jeans, she pulled out the strip of Life-Stills™. They were still wrapped in the accompanying literature, which she threw on the floor without a second thought. Sia peeled a sticker off the strip and looked at it as it sat on the tip of her index finger. It looked harmless... and useless.

She placed the sticker onto her tongue and felt it start to dissolve. It didn't taste of anything. Like paper, she thought, closing her eyes. She couldn't be sure if she had dozed off or not, but when she came to, she felt her body straighten out, her muscles becoming more... confident. Sia opened her eyes and stared at the ceiling, suddenly aware that she no longer felt sad or depressed. She actually felt... happy.

She sat up on the couch and looked around. She would usually cry at the sight of her flat after a nap, but now this thought bemused her. With her posture perfect, her head held high, she turned to look around some more, feeling like a stranger in her own flat. Sighting the strip of Life-Stills™ and its literature strewn on the floor, she recalled what she had just done.

She smiled.

This positive feeling seemed new and strange to her, even though she knew that was absurd. It brought back memories of when she was younger, memories of her graduation, of getting her first job, of meeting Marc, and of course, their wedding day. All the moments in her life when she was confident and happy. Having been given this moment of clarity in her thoughts, Sia tried to remember why she had been so depressed only ten minutes before. Why had she wanted to commit suicide so badly?

Her thoughts drifted to her wedding day, but the memories were patchy. The morning after the wedding, she found Marc in bed with her, cold. His corpse was slightly grey, his eyes open and lifeless. She remembered screaming and trying to close his eyes, but the skin of his eyelids was rigid. The memories flooded her mind, but she felt no emotional register. It was... just a memory.

A memory that she brushed aside easily now, as she got up and went towards the shower. She was very aware of her foul state.

Time passed quickly that afternoon for Sia. After she showered, she started unwrapping and putting away gifts, even drawing up an inventory of items. She kept working, her mind so fully concentrated on the task that she only stopped when her mother arrived.

Sia's mother, Tonje, having seen Sia in a complete state for nearly a month, was shocked to find her daughter up, showered, and doing household chores. The flat was tidy, and Sia looked pretty and normal.

Both women stared at each other, not knowing what to say. Sia broke the trance by smiling, which only made Tonje cry. They hugged for a long while, still not speaking, before Sia suggested that they go out for dinner. Tonje agreed and placed the groceries that she had brought with her — having planned to cook for her daughter as she had done every night after the incident — into the fridge.

"I can cook that tomorrow, mum. Thanks."

Tonje was still shaking with relief as they walked out of the flat into the night, heading quietly to Sia's favourite Italian restaurant across the road. There, Sia explained the concept of Life-Stills™, as her mother nodded in disbelief, while both spooned delicious risottos into their mouths.

Sia woke the next morning thinking about what had happened the previous afternoon. She knew that she was back to being depressed again; tears welled up in her eyes when she thought about how the bed was too big for just her. But now, she had a sense of determination within her. She wanted another dose of Life-Stills™.

She bolted out of her room, into the living room and frantically searched for the strip. Spotting it on the coffee table, she tumbled onto the sofa, grabbing the strip, and plucked a sticker, placing it straight onto her tongue without hesitation. Within moments, she felt the change come about again, quicker this time.

As she sat in the perfect state of confidence, calm, and clarity, Sia considered what she wanted to do that day. She knew that she had to get her life in order.

After a shower and breakfast, Sia pulled out the suitcase in her bedroom, which had remained shut since the wedding. It was packed for the honeymoon, which had never happened. They were supposed to have been on the beach in the Seychelles, sipping cocktails and working on their tans for two whole weeks. Marc's best friend, a travel agent, had helped them to book it, and it was he who had cancelled it that fateful day, and helped her get a full refund for the trip.

Unzipping the case, she found her bikinis, sundresses, a pair of jeans and some light tops. She didn't care for any of these, as it was now the start of autumn and the weather was getting chilly. She reached for the beautifully packed pouches that kept her toiletries, underwear, and some other bits and bobs. She was surprised at how little she could remember of what was in them.

As she unpacked the items, she organised them into piles based on where they needed to go; bathroom cabinet, wardrobe, laundry bag... it was simple, until she came across a small glass vial. That was when her phone rang.

It was Dr Holloway, checking in. Sia was distracted and wanted to get off the phone, but Clare was adamant that they meet, especially since Sia sounded so much better. Eventually, Sia agreed, if only to get off the phone. They would meet later that afternoon at the clinic.

Returning to the vial, Sia held it between her thumb and index finger, swirling the clear, slightly yellow liquid. What was it for? She couldn't remember, but she knew she must have used it, since it was half empty. Storing it somewhere safe, Sia tidied up the scattered bits and went to get ready for her meeting with Dr Holloway. Perhaps she could fill in another prescription of Life-Stills™ there.

≈

"You look amazing!" Clare reached out to hug Sia as she stepped into the doctor's office. "How do you feel?"

Feeling bewildered at the reaction, Sia managed to reply, "Normal, I guess."

"Who oversaw your first application?"

Sia realised that she hadn't followed any of the guidelines given, and decided to lie. "Oh, my mum."

"Great, I'll make an appointment to chat with Tonje soon." Clare scribbled and nodded to herself.

Sia didn't want that to happen, but she couldn't think of any excuses just yet.

"Do you remember anything more from the incident?"

"What incident?"

"Oh, it's worked really well, hasn't it? But, listen," Clare hesitated and leaned forward. "What we need to do, is to face what it was that made you ill in the first place, now that you are starting to feel better. Do you understand? It might be hard, but it's time. I'm going to have to ask you to try and remember exactly what happened at your wedding. And afterward." Clare gave Sia a moment to take in the message before asking, "Are you ready?"

"Oh. Of course. That makes sense."

Clare ushered Sia to a more comfortable chair in

the room. Sia's mind started to drift over all that had happened. She remembered the church. She remembered the beautiful readings by her best friend Adam, who had tried so hard to help her out during those dark days – she had pushed him aside instead, afterward. She remembered the reception, then, and the last night she and Marc had spent together.

"Tell me what you remember, Sia." Clare sat watching as Sia relayed what she could see; what she was starting to remember.

"I remember the night. Once everyone had left, Marc called for champagne and we sat in the bath together. It was... lovely." Sia's mind flashed forward to the next scene that night, after the bath, after they had made love, to when Marc was fast asleep. She remembered now. She remembered taking the glass vial. Meta-cyanide. It was a little fuller then, when she had twisted the top off and put just a few drops on Marc's lips. He had even smacked his lips together in his sleep, as if he had just tasted something nice.

Sia smiled.

"It must have been a beautiful night for the both of you," Clare said, reading the smile.

Sia nodded as she realised that she had planned it all along. Marc had taken out life insurance. If he were to die unexpectedly, in an accident, she would get the flat, as well as nearly two million pounds.

The smile on her lips stretched further.

"Tell me what happened, then."

"After the bath, we made love like never before. It was special, we were husband and wife. Then, I fell asleep in his arms." Sia continued smiling. Dr Holloway looked away, slightly embarrassed.

"Do you remember anything else after that?"

Sia shook her head. "No. Nothing happened." She altered her facial expression for the doctor's benefit, curling her mouth into a scowl, then a sneer as she shouted, "I woke up to find him dead!"

The room became quiet as Sia opened her eyes and looked into her lap, not trusting herself to look up at the doctor. Clare, concerned that she might have undone any progress, went to Sia to comfort her.

"It's OK, Clare," Sia said, still with a tinge of made-up sadness in her voice. "I'm glad I can see clearly now. I think… I think I can slowly learn to move on."

"That's great. That's really great. I'm so glad that we've made so much progress, Sia."

Sia nodded and pretended to put on a brave face.

"If you feel OK, then you won't need to continue taking Life-Stills™. You can take one once a week at the most, or whenever you feel the depression coming on. Otherwise, the best thing to do is to get your life back on track."

"I understand. Thanks, Clare."

The doctor left Sia with a few more bits of advice before letting her go. "Take care, Sia, and well done for your courage. Do let Tonje know that I'll be in touch soon."

~

At home, Sia found herself shaking, and she realised that she was excited. She felt driven to do something, but she wasn't sure what. She went to the living room and helped herself to one more dose of Life-Stills™, knowing that she wouldn't be needing them anymore after this.

As the chemicals washed through her body, her plan became clear. She reached for her phone and dialled her mother's number.

"Mum? What did you do with dad's insurance money after he died?"

Tonje, glad to hear Sia taking charge of her own life again, told her daughter that most of the money was placed in an old savings account that she'd put in both of their names after Sia had started working part-time in high school.

"That's really smart, Mum, so it's an account that we can jointly access, right?"

"Yes, that's why I picked it. If anything happened to me, you would have full access. And vice versa. The lawyer said that because the account has always been in both our names, you won't face any inheritance taxes when I'm gone."

"Wow. I hope I'll be able to make smart decisions like you did, mum."

"I'm sure you will. I'm so glad that you're able to move on, Sia, I just want to see you happy again."

"Thanks. I know, and I'm sorry that I put you all through so much grief.

Sia's mind went back to the small glass vial in her bedroom.

"Why don't you come around for dinner tonight, mum? I think I'm up for cooking."

First published in Mnemoscape, *Issue No. 2, March 2015.*

11

Ehta

There were two men huddled in a corner of a dark room, surreptitiously whispering even though there wasn't anyone else nearby. No one knew they were there, for they were Nowhere: a place that was found neither in time nor space. The room was small, a basic cube, and it sat within a bigger cube, and another, and another... They did not care about how many rooms there were; just knowing that each cube had a door that led further into Nowhere was enough.

They were talking about a professor who had snared their attention: Ueno Hidesaburo Sensei of the Imperial University. The Keepers of Darkness were not concerned about who this professor was. They just needed him taken care of. Their whispers scratched the air with static electricity for hours and days, but it did not matter, for they were Nowhere. As they concluded their machination, they knew that it was Ehta who would have to take on the job. She was patient and tidy, full of glam. She was also famous in her various guises and enjoyed fame.

She needed the fame to make her stronger. Already a demigod in different aspects, she had people talking about her, worshipping her, praying to her for all sorts. The two men knew that it was only a matter of time before she would be stronger than her oldest sibling, An.

~

1923, Tokyo

In the city that was buzzing with new technology — electricity — Ehta scoured the streets to find inspiration for a vessel, a new guise. The people were polite, soft-spoken and very organised. She did not fear men, for she knew that they were easy to control — as long as she did not make any mistakes. That was why she hated language. She always preferred to reach down to the essence of humanity, to its core, manipulating people's instincts instead. Words were too flimsy.

She saw her quarry, and she knew that it would be perfect. The bitch was already pregnant with seven pups. She would be the eight — an omen, definitely. Without hesitation, she approached the bitch as it whimpered in fear. Animals were always better at sensing her approach than humans, their instincts not blunted from ego and knowledge.

She reached into the bitch's mind, negotiating a safe passage across the planes. "In return," she told the bitch, "I will not hurt you, or any of your pups. You are not my concern today." The bitch complied and allowed her into her womb, as an eight-pup, ready to be delivered. It was only a two-day wait for Ehta before she saw sunlight through the eyes of a dog.

They nicknamed her "Kid Number Eight" — Hachiko. A golden-brown pup of the akita breed, Ehta relaxed in her first weeks in this new form and enjoyed being nurtured by the bitch. She knew she had time yet.

Ehta, as Hachiko, was nearly three months old when she strolled to Ueno Hidesaburo Sensei's home near Shibuya. An agriculture professor, she knew that the guise of a lost puppy was perfect in enticing him. Being a true gentleman, Ueno Sensei brought the pup to its rightful owner, and they exchanged some words about the inquisitive dog, Hachiko. Before the sun set on that fateful day, Hachiko returned with Ueno Sensei, etching the beginnings of the story that would be revered and repeated for generations to come. Hachiko the faithful dog has been adopted and had found its new, loving owner.

The next months were a tedious but necessary period for Ehta in collecting intelligence. Ueno Sensei was on the point of a breakthrough with his research on arable land, making headway in discoveries that would allow Japan to flourish as an agricultural country. His position at the Imperial University meant that his findings would reach the emperor's ears, were he less humble. His humility meant that he would share his research with no one, until he was sure of the results.

Without knowing it, he did share his work with someone, and that was Ehta, in the guise of Hachiko. The dog seemed intelligent to Ueno Sensei. Quick to learn of the professor's habits, the dog seemed to understand the professor's needs and sought to make his life easier and more comfortable. Proving itself to be a loyal companion, the dog followed Ueno Sensei to the train station every morning, a simple gesture to see him off to school, and waited at the station in the evenings for his return. Hachiko never missed a day.

What Ueno did not know was that Ehta was also monitoring intelligence from the Kempeitai, specifically the buntai that was currently based in Toba-shi in Mie prefecture. Shocho Kato Kenichii was setting up the new *Kempeitai* base that would prove to be the linchpin in a series of events seventeen years from then. This was what the Keepers of Darkness were protecting.

Every day, after Hachiko accompanied Ueno Sensei to Shibuya Station, the dog would head towards the marketplace where Ehta knew of a *Kempeitai* secret base. It was only ever manned by one officer at a time, as it was just a communications base. The officer would sit in a small shed at the back of a fruit stall and keep a radio switched to the *Kempeitai* band, noting down communications that were happening throughout Japan. Here, Hachiko would sit either inside the fruit stall or outside it, near the back, and listen in. The guise of a dog was coming in handy with its improved sense of hearing.

When the officer changed shifts, welcoming a new officer for the evening, Hachiko would know to head to Shibuya Station, to wait for Ueno Sensei like the faithful dog it was. This ritual went on for more than half a year before Ehta learnt of new developments.

The professor was anxious, excited about a new location that would help confirm his hypotheses. Ehta knew that it was in Toba-shi in Mie prefecture before he told her. Babbling at Hachiko every evening, Ueno Sensei boasted about his work to his only true companion, thinking nothing of it. But Ehta knew that it meant that it was time for her to take action.

For nearly another year, Ehta continued the Hachiko faithful dog ritual. Every morning, she would walk Ueno Sensei to Shibuya Station, and every evening, she would sit and wait for his arrival. At home, she would listen to his chattering about the day, but one thing changed.

As Ueno Sensei slept at night, Ehta would go to work. She would plant horrible dreams in his mind, dreams inspired by her colourful past in reaping souls, dreams that would slowly eat away his brains. A perfectionist, Ehta wanted the effects to be timed accurately, not too early nor too late.

In his dreams, Ueno Sensei saw what would be the future of the world, and the past so long ago that there was nothing but darkness, but he would not be able to make any sense of them. All he knew was that he was scared, more frightened than he ever was in his life. His biggest relief was when he awoke each time and saw Hachiko's sad dog eyes staring at him, as if it knew of his pain. Every morning, he would cuddle the dog and tell it of his dreams, and while Hachiko listened intently, even whimpering on cue, Ehta would laugh inside, basking in the glory of her success to come.

In April 1924, Ehta heard through the *Kempeitai* communications that a new troop member was initiated into its Toba-shi base. His name was Yamamoto Shuhei. It was this name that triggered her next steps, to complete her mission.

In May 1924, Ueno Hidesaburo Sensei died of a cerebral haemorrhage while lecturing a class. Hachiko had seen him to Shibuya Station in the morning, but he did not make it back that evening.

Ehta knew that the news of Ueno Sensei's death had to be suppressed in some way so that his colleagues would not pick up on his work, which would have been revolutionary. If found by the government, the success that the arable land research would bring would take priority over the need for a *Kempeitai* base — the need for Japan to postulate itself as a military power in the world when they could lead through agriculture and economy instead — which would bring about a change that would threaten history itself. And the Keepers of Darkness would not have that.

Ehta knew that the politics at the university would handle itself, since most professors would push for their own research to be made a priority before digging up a dead professor's work. However, she needed the general talk to move away from what the professor did. So she manipulated humanity at its core, as she had promised to do.

Ehta continued Hachiko's ritual, going to Shibuya Station every evening to wait for the dead professor who never returned. The community soon spotted the ritual and lapped it up. The talk went from the dead professor to the dead professor's loyal dog. His life and what he did were to be forever shadowed by the actions of his dog.

Even though Ehta knew that she was already successful in her mission, she kept up the ritual as she basked in her newfound fame as a dog. Realising the potential for another immortalisation, she played on for another nine years. This was long enough for the Kempeitai troop member Yamamoto Shuhei to be promoted to Chu-i, clearly on his way to becoming a Shocho within the next eight years.

Near the end of Hachiko's life, Ehta allowed herself to enjoy and reap the benefits of another successful mission, as she was pampered and worshipped by the community. Not knowing the full extent of her mastery, Ehta was confident that she would have acquired new followers as Hachiko that would strengthen her for a few years to come. She did not expect that she would be idolised and immortalised even a decade on. Her newfound fame and legend had pushed her above her siblings, giving her the ultimate position with the Keepers of Darkness.

∼

In the room within rooms, the scraping whispers of the two men huddled in the corner changed into croaky laughter, as they knew that the Darkness had been protected. From Nowhere, they opened a window to peer into the world that Ehta had been sent to preserve. It was December, 1941, in Japan.

Shocho Yamamoto Shuhei stood in a clean room in Toba-shi, with a telephone to his ear. As he confidently repeated the attack codes, the person at the end of the line stood baffled. Marshal Admiral of the Imperial Japanese Navy never thought that he would receive orders from a Shocho of the *Kempeitai*. However, the codes were accurate and the orders were clear.

Shocho Yamamoto Shuhei stood smiling as he heard the words, "Hai, wakarimashita". Hanging up the phone, he turned up his radio that was set to an American news station, waiting expectantly for news that the United States naval base Pearl Harbor had been destroyed.

12

Aquilae

To view the world from afar;
to accept what is seen and not mar
with subjective ideologies, the journey of the human race.

To learn to be individual,
accepting things that are factual
without enforcing representation through cultural malaise.

To be free and alone,
not have to worry or to hone
instincts, practices or superstitions on the surface.

To respect everybody
but not rely on anybody,
to neither love nor hate, but be neutral to every
face.

To resist fear,
to listen and hear
what each opinion, insult, compliment, really says.

To be able to see
that our ability to flee,
nurture, feed and struggle, is the ultimate grace.

To be humbled by the stars.

An earlier version was published in For Love and Poetry,
by Universe and Words, January 2013.

Thank you for reading

YOUR FREE STORY IS WAITING

Sign up for updates on new creative content by Yen, and get a free short story.

yenooi.com/freestory

About the Author

Yen Ooi started writing as an outlet for her wild imagination, which was instigated at a young age by her appetite for books. Having had a vibrant career in music touring, education, and project management, in 2008 Yen put her skills towards writing stories — producing speculative, fantasy, and science fiction in various guises. Yen is a member of ALLi and BSFA, and a member and panellist of Worldcon. She shares her home and writing lair in London with her patient husband and two mischievous cats.

Connect with Yen:

@yenooi

facebook.com/yenooi

yenooi.com